For *everyone* on our earth

- Anahita Teymorian

#TheresRoomforEveryone
#HopeinaScaryWorld

THERE'S ROOM FOR EVERYONE

This edition first published in the United States in
2019 by Tiny Owl Publishing Ltd.

www.tinyowl.co.uk

A CIP record for this book is available from the Library of Congress.

ISBN 978-1-910328-53-8

Printed in China

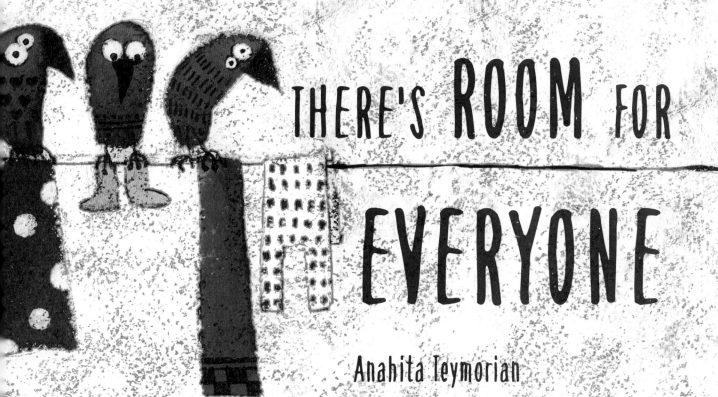

There's ROOM FOR EVERYONE

Anahita Teymorian

TINY OWL

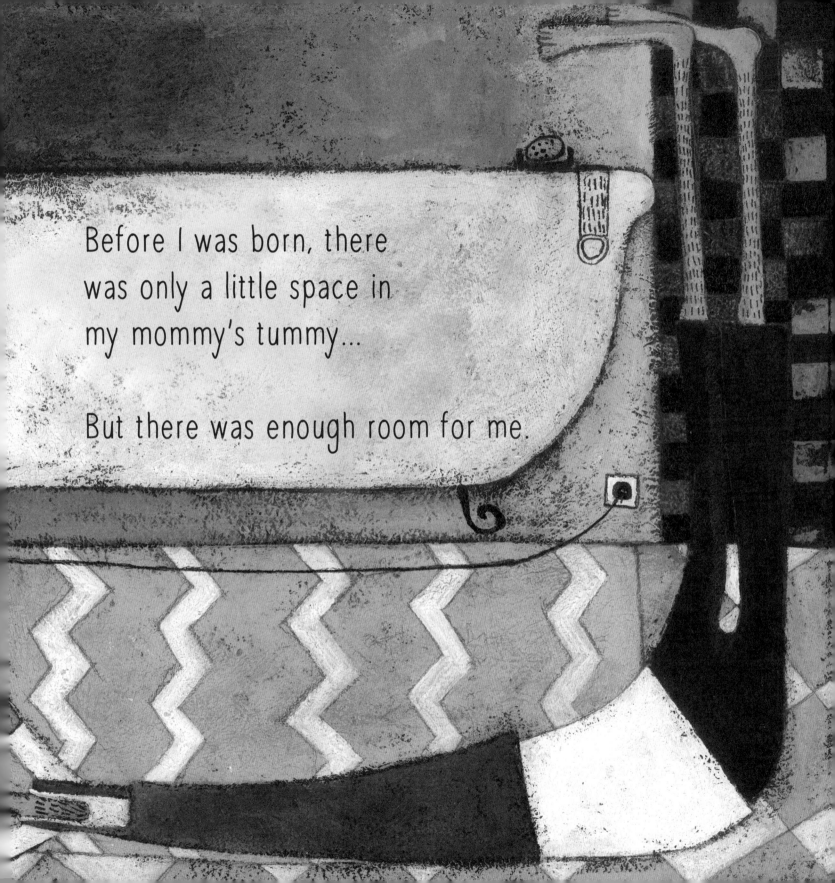

Before I was born, there was only a little space in my mommy's tummy...

But there was enough room for me.

When I got **bigger,** our house seemed smaller...

But there was enough room for all of us.

There was even enough
room for all my toys!

At night, when I looked up to the sky, there was enough room for all the stars... even the moon!

In the morning, I saw there was room
for all the birds in the garden.

And when I went to the library, there was room for all the books I wanted to read.

FAUST
HAMLET
Don Quixote
Les Miserables
self_Knowledge
Divine comedy
care for the world
Iliad & odyssey-Homer
I am a human
tle prince
STORY
ld or our world

When I grew up, I became a sailor and went to explore the world. I saw there was room in the sea for all the fish. Even the whales!

Wherever I went, there was enough room for all the animals. Even the giraffes and elephants!

But as I traveled the world,
I saw people everywhere
fighting for space.

Small spaces.

BIG SPACES...

Strange

spaces...

Now that I'm older and have learned more
about the world, I have a secret
I want to share with you...

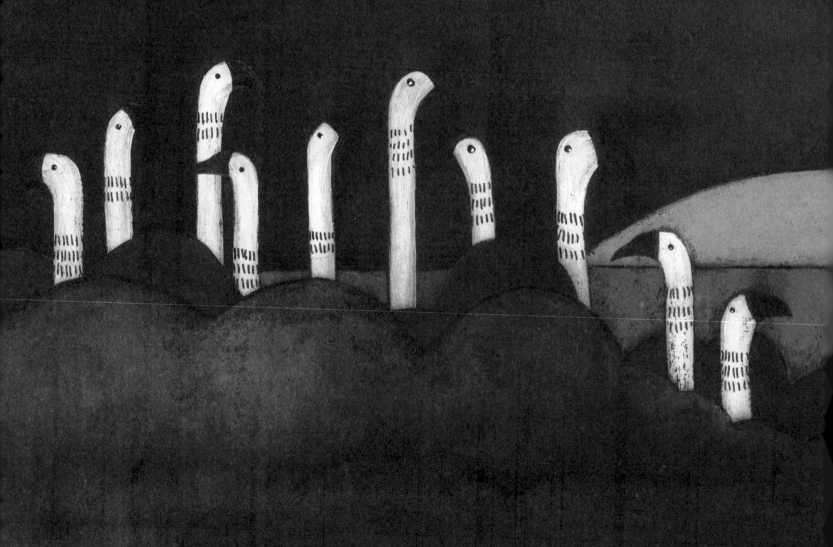

If we are kinder, and if we love each other then,
in this beautiful world, there's room for everyone.

A message from Anahita

One day, fed up with all my chores, I collapsed in front of the TV on the sofa and took a huge bite out of my sandwich. As usual, the news on the TV was showing people fighting each other for a piece of land...a piece of planet Earth. Suddenly I wasn't hungry anymore, and I put the rest of my sandwich on the table in front of me.

The table was full of toys, books, and dirty plates from the day. But, amazingly, my sandwich found a place on it too. And then, as usual, I started to argue with the TV. I was angry with it and with the people on it. I pointed to them and began shouting, "Why don't you stop it? Why are you never happy? Stop being greedy. Believe me! There's enough room for all of you. Look at the sky, look at the sea, look at the jungle. No, just look at my table!"

Then I went to my room and wrote down all of the things I'd said to the TV on paper. That's how "There's Room for Everyone" started. I remember that night, when I went back to rest on the sofa, the TV was still showing news of war everywhere. And the cat was eating the leftovers of my sandwich.

Anahita Teymorian lives with her cat and daughter in the city of Tehran, Iran. Anahita's books are known all over the world, and her work has been featured in major international exhibitions.